The Worst Hero
Part I

The Rise of Germania

By

Kevin James Donoghue

The Alchemy Series

A 5th Worlde Saga

1st edition

A note from the author

The Great Book of Alchemy is a collection of sagas from the 5th Worlde. These sagas are not a series of historical novels, and whilst many of the characters have indeed appeared in the history of your world ~ in the 5th Worlde ~ their histories are completely different and a substantial amount of imagination has been used to ensure this fact.

The Bells of the Watch

Number of Bells	Bell Pattern	Middle Watch	Morning Watch	Forenoon Watch	After-noon Watch	Dog Watch First	Dog Watch Last	First Watch
one	1	0.30	4.30	8.30	12.30	16.30		20.30
two	2	1.00	5.00	9.00	13.00	17.00		21.00
three	2 1	1.30	5.30	9.30	13.30	17.30		21.30
four	2 2	2.00	6.00	10.00	14.00	18.00		22.00
five	2 2 1	2.30	6.30	10.30	14.30		18.30	22.30
six	2 2 2	3.00	7.00	11.00	15.00		19.00	23.00
seven	2 2 2 1	3.30	7.30	11.30	15.30		19.30	23.30
eight	2 2 2 2	4.00	8.00	12.00	16.00		20.00	24.00

The Worst Hero
Part I

The Rise of Germania

1

Yellow River

The Warlord and his companions; The Knight Templar Rembald de Voczon, the Polo Brothers, and Prester John the Holy Man, along with their party, are being pursued across the plains of Great Russia. They are located near the eastern bank of the Volga.

It was one of those rare nights. The forest was quiet and still and only the sound of our horses disturbed the peace. We exited the darkness of the tree-line and emerged into the small clearing. Ackus, my faithful mount, breathed heavily as I pulled him up and I heard his hooves squelch in the soft, rain drenched ground.

The moon hung in the sky. Just there. Gigantic, red, and staggeringly low. Just there ~ on the edge of the night. And it felt as if you could touch it by simply raising a finger. It filled the whole night; flooding the world with its presence and its strange tint. I studied it with a long gaze as the other riders passed me.

The men rode in pairs; each man leading two or three horses. Most of the packhorses were heavily laden with large wooden crates. They were fastened to either side of the animals to maintaining a balance.

Prester John and the Templar reined in beside me. We sat silently contemplating that moon. The Templar raised his hand and grabbed at the moon. The Prester laughed loudly and shook his head in disbelief.

'Fool!'

Sir Rembald smiled softly as he soothed Hades, his pale mare; all the while whispering softly to her as he patted her neck. The tension that had grown between us over the last few days was broken.

'The sun will turn to darkness…and the moon to blood before the great and terrible day of the Lord shall come.' Quoted Prester John.

'Indeed Holy Man? But is this not also a sign that some great change is also coming?' I asked.

The Prester smiled as he loosened and removed his helm. He dragged a cloth square across his sweaty, bald head.

'Oh my friend…the scriptures…they say that the Bloode Moon occurs as a sign that the end of days is upon us. I think there can be no bigger change to our world than that. It is an omen.' He spat at the ground.

'…And one that is known for the storms that often accompany it. Storms like the one we encountered this afternoon. And yet…we both knew we were damned long ago. Did we not?'

He smiled his crooked yellow-toothed smile at me and replacing his helm. Then he kicked his horse on to a trot and followed the men as they re-entered the forest at the far side of the clearing.

'In my country...it would be considered a good omen. And the Gods know how much we needed one!' Said the Templar in his matter of fact way before he followed the Holy Man across the clearing.

I stroked Ackus's neck as I continued to stare at that dark red moon. I regarded it for a few more moments then I too reached to touch it. I cursed under my breath at my stupidity and flicked my heels on to Ackus' flanks urging him onwards again.

I rode steadily under the shadow of that Bloode Moon and stared blankly at the night. Time seemed to stretched ahead of me as my thoughts tumbled over each other; like a child's boat in a mountain stream.

It seemed to take me an eternity to cross that clearing. And yet in reality only a few moments had passed before I again entered the dark forest.

The forest stretched along the lowland plain that bordered the edge of the Yellow River. The country was wild and that hid our passage from those eyes that searched after us.

I could had sworn that I felt her gaze fall on me. Occasionally I saw her face in the shadows. She laughed at me from the darkness there. At other times I could feel her eyes as they crawled across my skin. Eyes that were hunting us...hunting me ~ Wu's eyes.

And soon, without any given command but by a common urgency, we all began to move just that little bit faster until after only a few heartbeats we were racing along the dark road, under the shade of the pine trees, as if the devil himself where chasing us.

Ackus lay his ears up as the wolves howled for the first time that night. The hunt was on again. I had counted that we were now only a company of ten and eight. The Templar, Prester John and their knights, the Italian brothers, Lady Ju who carried the baby and me. There were twenty and one extra horses and they carried the boxes. But each night we lost another horse and sometimes two to those damned wolves or they fell broken legged to the roots of this eternal dark forest.

We had fled Old Cathay, an organised, purposeful unity. We had ridden with pride in our gleaming armour. There had been forty of us and a further twenty and eight horses. In truth it had been a long hard journey. And as we fled we had perished, and we had perished, and we had perished again.

And still I had expected that too. For the Empress Wu was not the kind of person who gave up easily. Not the kind who gave up at all. And whatever the outcome ~ she would never forgive me. No; she was not the type of woman who ever forgave and I knew that her vengeance would be swift. At first it would be filled with an awesome anger. Then it would become cold. More calculate. Deliberate. Wu ~ she would study how to bring about her revenge. And finally. It would be abominable and terrible to behold.

And after all; we had stolen the greatest treasure from her. A treasure that was more valuable to her than all the gold in the world. And in truth I did not care anymore; for I was going home.

2

The Wrath of Gods

The Warlord and his companions; The Knight Templar Rembald de Voczon, the Pole Brothers, and Prester John the holy man, along with their party, are being pursued across the plains of Great Russia. They are located near the eastern bank of the Volga.

We had passed through the great wall and suddenly our journey became easier. Though I knew that Wu's men would soon be pursuing us. Still now the imminent threat came from the Mongol armies that roamed the plains plundering and raiding the caravanserai.

Passing through the wall had been far easier than I anticipated. A guilty man may think that it was too easy. Of course I had taken great care with the planning and we had acted with a practised speed. We had reached the gate before the news of our crime. Indeed, before anyone was aware that a crime had even been committed. And no one had dared to question the Warlord's warrant of office.

I knew that if our luck held; the news of our desertion should not reach the wall for several days. Everything depended upon how long the Empress dawdled at the Temple of Beauty. I knew my lover. And I was counting on her renowned vanity to aid us in our venture.

Still, Wu was ever present. I felt her searching after me with her scrying ball. Her spirit was haunting me in the dark of the night. Her face forever dancing through my dreams. She lurked in the very shadows. Cursing me as I rode passed. And I knew too that her men would be following us. As in time so would she herself.

Yes, Wu would follow me. Her retribution would be something to behold. I shuddered as I thought about it and looked over my shoulder for a glimpse of her. Nothing, just more shadows. Still I had lived with retribution before. And I had fled from it previously.

That last time; I had fled from the west to east but now the situation was reversed. Previously; I had sought only to escape the situation. Now; I had to escape Wu vengeance. For I had stolen the most precious treasure that Wu possessed. Oh yes! She would follow…follow me to the ends of the earth if need be. I would be luck if I ever escaped her reach. And I knew that.

Her predatory hands cradled the east; manipulating the nobles and the peasants a like. Even the Gods, on their high mountains, were not safe from Wu's ambition.

Her reach stretched further west than anyone ever realised. We of the west were unaware of her. They thought her irrelevant. The fools ~ they did not realise that her eyes encompassed the wealth of their kingdoms.

And Wu; She hated the gweilo. The 'White Devils' she called them. The Pale Ghosts. And I was counting on that. I may, just may, be able to deflect her wrath by focusing her attention on a greater, an all encompassing, wealth.

A cloud floated across the moon and the forest fell dark. Ackus shivered; I whispered encouragement to him before we continued through this never ending forest.

Wu; She had loved me. 'My Pale Ghost' she called me. Yes…she had loved me and I had betrayed that love. She loved to run her fingers over my body and stroke my gweilo skin. And yet she despised those fools who sat upon their little island and believed that they could control the whole world.

She laughed at them. She told me;

'They think that a women is a weak thing. An empty vessel. A trifle to be bargained in politics. A gift for a marriage bed. And they believed that they have an absolute, Gods given right, to rule the world.' She laughed aloud again. A laugh with a golden ring to it. A laugh her council feared. A laugh that could, so easily, turn into a snarl.

'Those Pale Ghosts…with their Holy Men. True Gods! They claimed…they claim that their Gods rule over and above our Gods.' She placed a piece of sugared sweetmeat in my mouth.

'…and their Far East Company [incorporating India and Siam] who dared to make their demands on me; The Empress. They dare to demand the right to flood my empire with opium. My empire!' Wu threw her goblet across the room. It was collected by a eunuch.

'I have no knowledge of their Gods, no reason to love their Gods. Do we not have Gods of our own.' She sneered and took a new goblet from the servant.

'They really have no idea of how we work. How the east works. None at all. And no idea of the awesome power we can wield.'

And what she meant of course was; the awesome power she could wield.

'It is my destiny to rule. I am the first female ruler of the Oriental Empire. The Empress of the whole of

Old Cathay. Have I not been told by my wizard? Seen it with my own eyes? Seen it in in my mystical objects.' She maintained that;

'The sooner that these Normans…these gweilo learned their lessons; the less harsh their disappointment will taste in their mouths. They think that they can just take. Take without permission. Take without consequence. They do not realise that they are putting their hand into the hornet's nest.' More snarling followed.

There was a saying in the east;

'The sun, the moon, and all the stars, would have been swallowed long ago…had they ever been so foolish to have fallen within the Empress's reach.'

And Wu? She was no ordinary woman. For she was a Goddess, and not only a Goddess but also a terrible dark sorceress. And I had been her lover, her warrior, her trusted assassin. And now…now she would deem me to be her mortal enemy. And worse, a thief. A thief of the worst kind. And she would hate me as only a woman can.

3

Here Comes The Man

Milo Bauermann; is the Warlord's man and has been recently appointed to the Imperial Guard. He is based at the castle of Hrad Devín which stands on a rocky precipice, over looking the river Danube, high in the north-eastern Alps and deep in the heart of the Holy Roman Empire. His duty is to protect the boy Prince, Rudolf, with his own life.

A midnight dark had spread across the land and a fresh mist swirled in the gentle wind. It was a chilly night. I dreamed of home and the warm fire that had always danced in the heath. I waited for the Warlord.

With a clatter of hooves the riders entered the keep. A giant of a man dismounted from his black stallion. Hot breath oozed from the horse's nostrils ~ like steam rolling upwards from a boiling kettle. The great beast's hooves stamped on the cobbles of the courtyard and he released a furious stream of piss. It spurted like a sluice across the cobbles and mixed with the mud, muck, and straw.

Hrad Devín sat solidly on a rocky precipice. It looked down on the river Danube that swirled around its roots, as it flowed from the north-eastern alps. The castle was a wide low building. It massive walls that surrounded the inner courtyard of the high bailey and the mighty bastion.

The Warlord adjusted his sword and removed his helmet. He gently stroked the neck of the horse and whispering something softly to him, as he handed the reins to the stable boy.

‘Make sure he is well fed and watered. We leave with the sun.’ He snapped.

The lad led Ackus to the stables. Captain Johannus and I waited in silence.

‘Bring me to the Prince. I have news.’ He ordered.

And we did.

The wind was blowing hard and fresh off the mountains and it swept through the heavy woven cloths that acted as curtains in the keep. The torches flickered and sputtered as we approached the door which stood at the end of the long dark corridor. Two Imperial Guards stood on duty at the door. They were both huge blonde warriors with bulging muscles. They wore only simple ring mail over there leathers and the whole ensemble was covered by their white tabard, upon which ~ place over the heart ~ sat a double headed black eagle on a field of Gules. Both wore a wide black leather belt that wrapped around their waist and upon which rested a long sword and an ever-sharp dagger.

The sentinels recognised us as we approached. They clasped their spears to their expansive chests and moved them to a vertical position. Then they stood aside to let us pass. The Warlord rapt twice upon the door. Hardly gentle. He entered without waiting to be invited.

It was a large chamber, one that contained many silk and woven fabrics and furnishings of a solid dark wood. There was a grand sleeping couch which was covered with deep soft furs, a scribing table, and several low couches. Bookcases lined the walls and each was stacked to the ceiling.

I had never seen so many books. I wondered who could possibly read them all. Did one life time contain enough moments? The cost of the candle alone would ruin most families!

The room was well lit. Large candles and torches, that where held in metal sconces, where mounted high upon the walls. A stone chiselled fireplace was set into the end wall and a bright fire roared in the hearth. There room had only one window but it had a small balcony and looked out across the valley. It was almost a league straight down to the river which flowed at the bottom of the cliff.

'Highness, I have sad news. Your brother has died.' The Warlord said in his simple clipped, matter of fact, way.

The young boy Prince was seven and he almost looked it. He was short for his age. His hair was as black as a ravens and it fell down to his shoulders. Straight and smooth; with not a curl insight. His eyes were dark too; wide set, and there was a slight flatness to the bridge of the nose. And just for a moment, in the flickering half-light of the candles, he looked a little more Russian than truly of High Österriech.

'Otto? How did he die?'Asked the young boy as he tilted his head slightly to one side. He picked up a black knight from the marble chess board.

'It was a sudden illness, Highness. A flux of the bowel.'

'That is sad.'

'Yes, Highness…but now we must prepare. All is ready.' The Warlord moved across the room.

'Will all of Germania now be mine?' He enquired meekly.

The Warlord stood over to the map table. His finger

moved quickly across the map.

'First the west, then the north, after; these, the major Principalities. The remaining small states…here and here…they will submit, and willingly too. We will bully some…and bribe the others…with land, marriages and money.'

A finger purposefully stabbed at the map following each statement.

'Here and here…they will resist us…at first; for a while…and yet in the end…victory! It will be inevitable. And finally…' His finger came to rest on a small group of islands in the wild northern seas.

'That which may not wish to be ours…we will take.' The mighty warrior said without hesitation.

'My spies tell me that they have just lost a mighty piece ~ their Witch Queen.' The boy strode back to the chess table and lifted the piece. He twirled it in his fingers.

'They grow weaker as we grow strong…no?' The Prince asked in his clipped manor.

'They do indeed, Your Grace. I see that you have been studying your lessons. That is good.' The Warlord smiled softly at the boy. It was a side of him that I had not perviously seen.

'But now…come, Highness. It is time to sleep. The High Priest and his acolytes are waiting for us. We leave with the sun. I would have you ride with Milo here. Dress as a simple soldier…in your mail and leather. It will hide you from our enemies…and disguise you from the Eunuch's spies. It's a safer way to travel. Tomorrow our great venture begins.'

The young man moved over to the map table and lay the black queen across those small Islands. He nodded his head. Together the Warlord, the Captain, and I left the room.

4

And It Came To Pass

The Warlord; and his companions, The Knight Templar, Rembald de Voczon, the Polo Brothers, and the Holy Man; Prester John, along with their party are being pursued across the plains of Great Russia. They are located near the eastern bank of the Volga.

On the Journey we had skirted the main centres of population and they were sparse enough on the Great Planes but it was impossible to cross here without that passing been known by the tribes. And the Silk Road itself is a treacherous hotbed of rumour and gossip. At each bend, pass, river crossing, and caravanserai along the way, death lay in ambush for us.

I had learned of the Mighty Khan's plans to lead his army north for the summer. He was to campaign along the boarders of the Great Russia's. And this had hastened my own plans. The opportunity to pass through the plains unmolested was far too good to miss. And praise be to the Gods; we had managed to evade all but a few of his patrols.

On the third day, of the second week, we meet a large patrol in a high ridged pass. It was led by a grisly old bear of a Mongol.

We had come across each other as the sun rose

high towards the noon and they; returning from their own campaigns. They consisted mainly of young boys and wounded men. They were weighed down with as much plunder as we ourselves were.

Their leader looked annoyed. He was disturbed that he had encountered us without being warned by his scouts. I grinned to myself as I saw that thought on his face. We had left those scouts laying amongst the rocky outcrops, smiling long red smiles or clutching at an belly full of arrows.

The truth was that my men were far more dangerous than his. Each of them knew that our theft would mean a huge rewards for them if we escaped and certain death if we did not.

Their leader was travel stained. The dust of the road lay heavy upon his furs. He wore only a plain leather helm. He carried a small round shield, a curved edged sword, and had a bow slung over his shoulder. He halted his horse at the top of the pass. We in turn halted at the bottom. We studied each other for a few moments.

The sun passed behind a cloud and reappeared again seemingly stronger, harsher, than before and with each heartbeat that passed the sweat on my brow grew heavier. I could see that he had mounted archers in his force. Archers who could draw and shoot three arrows as quickly as a horse could move a dozen lengths. And they were above us. They had the advantage of the high ground. Then again, we were all well armoured and had bigger, stronger, and faster horses.

The sun glanced off a puddle of water, high on the left of the trail which glimmered as it reflected back. It looked like a solid piece of gold; half buried in the rocks.

'We could rush them.' I said to the Templar and Prester John as they drew their mounts up on either side of me.

'There is no need.' Said Prester John.

'See with your eyes, hear with your ears. The Gods have given you these gifts. His men are made up of the injured and the young. The sun is in his eyes. He will want no conflict here.' He finished.

Rembald de Voczon said nothing. He stroked the neck of Hades gently and smiled his crooked smile. Then his fingers loosened his sword in its sheath and he placed his conical helm over his coif and adjusted it; lowering the nasal stem. The Prester caught his glance and announce:

'You know my order forbids me to draw blood with a blade during combat. I will ride with our lady and give her what protection I can.'

He patted the spiked mace that was slung across his saddle. I gave the signal to proceed in single line. I took the head of the column urging Ackus forward at a slow walk.

The Templar followed immediately to my rear and moved easily to my left side. The Mongol Captain watched us as me moved. His keen eyes searching out our intent; knowing full well that if we charged his force, in single file, that his archers could only take one or two of us before we were upon him. He nodded his head and urged his horse forward to meet us. His warriors fell in to a single line behind him.

And so it was that we drew together in the pass. The Mongol force travelling downhill and we in our turn moving upwards to meet them. Each step, that our horses took, was a move closer towards life or death. The very air in the pass became stifled and strained.

I watched, peculiarly distracted, fascinated as a bead of sweat dropped from my nose on to the neck of Ackus. I could smell the scent of wild thyme in the air. I steadied my stead and patted him on the neck. I could feel the warmth of his body radiating through the soft inner leather part of my mailed gauntlet. I became strangely aware of my own solitude in that instant. And that of the young life that I was sworn to protect.

The piercing cry of a hawk broke the moment. It soared so high above the world. Black against the noonday sun. It hovered high above the pass.

The moment shattered; like a wave upon the rock's of my coastal homeland. The sound of the horses and their heavy loads flooded back into my senses. We creaked and clanked our way forward. Step by agonising step. We move inevitably towards each other.

Soon, so very soon, I could see the yellow specks in his dark, soulless eyes. I could almost taste the wild garlic on his breath.

We met halfway along the path. He looked straight into my eyes. I could tell he was studying my face and I saw his look. I could almost hear the cogs whirling; like those I had seen when I had visited Su Song, the Royal Astronomer. When he had shown me his amazing clock tower. He called it a cosmic engine.

Yes, the Mongol Captain had seen me. And he was registering my mixed heritage. My strange epicedian eyes of dazzling blue. The long sleek blonde hair with the heavy drooping moustache. And the fact that I wore no beard. He had noticed my pale European skin; white but tanned a deep dark reddish brown. And I knew then that his report would dam us forever.

That was the moment that I decided he must die. I gave Ackus a swift flick of my heals and pulled on the rains. He dance forward moving automatically to the right and upwards. Ackus knew what to do.

He reared and let his hooves rake the breast of the
Mongol's horse, and he trumpeted loudly, his yellow
teeth snapping ferociously at the other horses face.
In comparison to our horses the Mongol's step bred
horses were a far smaller breed and Ackus, in particular, was several hands bigger than them. Yet still
the captain rode a sturdy beast. It was well trained
and it took all of Ackus's inherent brutality to scare
him. But Ackus did scare him. And eventually the
Captain's horse reared and pulled off to its left in
fright.

This, of course, left the Mongol leader with his
right shoulder and neck exposed and his sword and
shield on the wrong side of his body. Turning Ackus
swiftly to my left again I urged him forward; all the
while drawing Empress's Kiss from her sheath. One
swift continual movement. Like I had done a thou-
sand times before. That single sweep continued and
slashed right; across my body at the gap between his
head and his shoulder armour.

Empress's Kiss flashed sharply, drank deeply, and
sent a spray of blood upwards in an arc. It pumped
with every heartbeat. The Captain's head fell, spin-
ning from his shoulders.

Plunging Ackus forward I was on the second man
before the head of the Captain had hit the ground.
Thrusting straight this time; using the point of my
curved sabre. Empress's Kiss pierced him between
the lower helmet guard and the medallion at the top
of his chest. She slipped smoothly straight through
his neck leaving a long thin oval cut, which welled
slowly red, as the man drowned in his own blood.

I watched abstractedly as the Templar sped passed
me on Hades. I saw the Captain's head as it rico-
cheted off the wall of the pass and danced between
the horse's forelocks. Rembald took the third man.
And the forth. Ackus veered left and forward as an

arrow sailed passed. I felt my blade strike the bone of the archer's arm; just below the elbow.

The middle of the Mongol column was now backing into its own rear guard and we were on them. My men finished them quickly; dropping the last few with arrows as they abandoned their cargo and fled backwards, up the pass.

The hawk circled my head. It let out another piercing cry. It rang clean and clear; like a bell does. It reverberated off the high walls of the pass; as if it were announcing the end of the combat.

I dismounted at the top of the pass and looked at the carnage that I had sown. Kneeling, there in a small ledge-like clearing, I said a silent prayer for the dead. We carried the bodies to the top of the pass and cutting a shallow grave placed them together. The men built a small cairn of boulders and rocks to cover the grave and protect it from wild scavengers.

Prester John said the words of his God. While we worked the Lady Ju held the baby tightly to her breast. He guzzled greedily; blissfully unaware of the death that I had wrought for his sake.

We had lost only two men. Though in truth I didn't like the look of one of our injured; his wounds looked bad to me and I silently counted him as the third.

We had captured eleven of their horses and the men were cheerful, as all soldiers are after an easy victory, and they rummaged through the booty that we had gained.

The view from the top of the pass was good. We could see that our way lay clear in all directions and that we were in no immediate danger. So, after the burials , we took the time to take our ease and have a small lunch. I watched the others eat their lunch of hard cheese and stale bread whilst I cleaned my sword with a soft oiled rag that I kept in my saddle-bags.

I thought of Wu again. Empress's Kiss had been made by her finest 'smiths. It is essentially a Dao sword. It was given to me by the Empress herself as a declaration of our love. The sword had been specially forged and adapted to my western style of fighting. She was longer than the celestial swords, by a third again, and had a broad sharp blade with both a double edge and point. She flared in a curve upwards towards the point. This gave her a vicious hooked lip, that made the back swing as deadly as the fore. The length of the blade shimmered in the sun. It gleamed; for the blade was imbued with magical properties. The Warlock had bathed her in an enchanted acid bath and when the 'smith had withdrawn her the sword had been magically covered with scrolls and symbols. Sometimes I could see the image of the same 'Red Dragon' that Wu's Wizard had tattooed upon my right forearm. It was the same as that the men of the tongs, that were controlled by Wu in the hell like city of Hong Kong, also wore. It was her mark. She had stamped it into my skin. Declaring me to be her belonging!

I eased the cloth down the length of the blade, caressing the folds and I watched the Lady Ju with the babe. I could not help but wondered about Wu. Was it true? Does love eventually fade away and die?

5

The Priory of Saint Florian

Milo Bauermann; is with the Warlord and his party, who are journeying west towards Bavaria in the heart of Germania. Milo has been designated to protect the young Prince Rudolf who is dressed as a page and rides at his side.

It was mid-afternoon and the sun shone down upon the rain soaked road. Its reflection glimmering brightly in the large puddles that had formed in the mire of the hard worn earth. We were a band of twenty and one men. We travelled purposefully along the narrow country roads. The hooves of our mounts squelched in the mud. The mud in turn splashed up their fetlocks and stained the bottom of our heavy cloaks. We turned the bend and the low sun blinded my eyes; dazzling. A bright autumn sun. The valley floor was covered by a sparse forest and, here and there, golden fields stretched down towards a distant river. The river was just visible to our right. It flowed quickly down from the mountains to join the swelling Danube.

Our descent from the mountains had taken two days and was always hard on the men and the mounts alike. Still; now the going was easier and the

countryside was more gentle and peaceful. There
would be a good crop this year; if the rains let up and
did not ruin the harvest.

We had been told that our journey was westward
and would take about nine days. We were travelling
light by means of the back roads and the small towns
and villages. We avoided the city of Salzburg entirely.
We spoke to no one and no one spoke to us. Quite the
contrary; whenever we came upon a wagon or cart
the merchants and the peasants alike would scowl
and hide their eyes from us. I smiled to myself know-
ingly. I had seen scared people before.

Although I was only twenty I was now a man of ex-
perienced and had been soldiering for the best part
of five years. I had fought my way from Hesse across
the Germanic Principalities. Oft times I was on the
winning side but it was true that I had been on the
losing side a few times too.

However; fortune like the lady she is had continued
to smile on me and I had only collected a broken arm,
a handful of scars, and lost no more than half an eye-
brow with a few chunks of my dirty brown hair.

And now I had been chosen by the Warlord himself. I had joined the Imperial Guard. I was to ride in
the escort of the young Prince. I knew that my lot
in life was improving. This was a far better life than
that of my brothers; clearing the forest, ploughing
the dark heavy soil, and sowing the sparse crops.
Crops that would fail in the heavy rains. And fail in
the dry heat of the summer sun. And fail in the cold
of the winter snows. Forever chasing the milk cows
and the sheep; out across the meadows. And digging
the turnips, the parsnips, swedes, and endless bloody
cabbages!

The farm was small and the family large. There
was not enough land to feed us all. And since mother
had died; father had struggled with the homestead.

I had been glad when the recruiting sergeant had appeared with his piper, drummer, and standard-bearer. He offered ready money, regular meals, and adventure. Both my brother Ziggy and I had enlisted. We had marched out of the valley with pride. Father had bid us a tearful farewell. Although he was losing cheap labour I expect he was glad to be rid of two ever hungry mouths. Osanna, my little sister, had run half a mile as she waved goodbye to us. I often wondered if I would ever see her again.

Ziggy and I had separated after the battle of Bronhöved; where we had won a famous victory. I had been injured. My arm had been broken in a cavalry charge. Squashed by a horses hoof. Ziggy, like an excited fool, had volunteered to joined the Hessian Brigade and fight for the English in the Colonies of the New World; induced by the huge rewards and the promise of his own land.

And now I was the Warlords' man. An Imperial Guard. Someone to be respected. Life was harder perhaps but better paid. And the girls! Well…all the girls admire a scar and they love a soldier. Especially Freya. I closed my eyes, smiled for a second, and felt Drake's rhythm jogging me gently as I envisaged Freya climbing up on top of me again. Big, blonde, and buxom, Freya…she knew how to make a man happy.

The brown gelding pulled on his bridle; waking me from my daydream. I watched as a flock of birds soared upwards from the small grove on the left. They flew low and swiftly across the field.

'Smelt a fox, eh boy. Or is it a boar?' I gently stroke Drake's neck as the horse neighed and shook his mane.

'Steady now.' I said as I patted his neck some more.

Ahead I could see the Warlord and the Outremer and I wondered what adventures they were leading us towards. The Outremer was new to the castles retinue. He styled himself Sir Johannus Von Württemberg. He was a grey, grizzled man and aged somewhere between forty and fifty years. Yet he was still firm of body and well muscled. He was an experience man at arms. His skin was that dark mahogany colour that is distinctive of all those who have recently returned from the crusades. He had fought at Acre with the famous Grand Master, Sir Henry de Walpot. And he had entered King Henry the Lions' service at the battle for Sicily.

We were moving at a careful pace. Faster for a while, then slowly for a few leagues. We rested the horses as they needed it. No one had been told of our destination but we carried enough provisions for nearly two weeks. As a company we carried many weapons. Far more than we really needed. Enough for fifty men or maybe more. Enough for a small war. There where swords, battle axes, morning stars, and daggers. The pack horses carried spears, bec de corbin, halberds, crossbows, and curved bows, with sheaths of arrows and bundles of bolts. Still we ourselves were lightly armoured and had little personal baggage.

The Danube was on our right now. So we must be heading west. I breathed deeply as we sat around the camp fire that evening and inhaled the smell of the rabbit as it sizzled. It's juices spit at the fire. It was rather to close to the flame's and was roasting to quickly. The men were all to hungry to cook it properly. After a time the conversation turned to speculation; as is usual with the common soldier.

'I'm no map reader...'

'That's the truth.' Interjected Wilf.

'...but there is talk of war with the little Prince of Liechtenstein...and that has to be somewhere over this way.' I said.

Wilf, the big shaggy Saxon, laughingly replied:

'Every where is somewhere, Ox Brain!'

He always called me that and he knew that I resented it. Dagmar chipped in from behind his shaggy beard.

'It's those heathen Turks again or maybe the Mongols.' He said.

He was slowly rubbing bacon grease into his long blonde hair. He had spent the last hour carefully platting it into two pigtails.

'Do all you Danes smell like breakfast or is that how you get the boys to suck your cock?' Asked Wilf.

We all laughed. Dagmar grinned slowly. His eye's sparkled dangerously for a moment and then the grin spread into a smile, and he joined in and laughed too.

'The boys suck my cock because it the biggest thing they have ever seen. Here, do you want to look? It's bigger than any of your damned sausages.'

He continued to laugh as he un-laced his breeches and took out his immense cock. He then started to swing it around in a circle, widdershins. Dagmar was easily the tallest of all the Komrades and even by our standards he was a massive man; in every sense. He was from the Kingdom of Danemark, somewhere in High Norway or Scandia. The story changed with every telling. He too had been at Bronhöved. He loved to boast about all the young men and the boys that he had captured in battle and then sexually brutalised before slitting their throats and kissing them lovingly. He would then hold them in a close embrace and rock them gently, like a little child, as they died. The 'Kiss of Death' he called it.

'We are going west; not east.' I told him.

'Put that thing away. I have not eaten yet! And I don't want to get it confused with my supper.' Complained Sir Johannus as he walked up to the fire.

'Milo; you will take the first watch. Wake Wilf at four bells. And you…' He nodded at Dagmar, who was hurriedly re-lacing himself.

'You…Vikingr, you can have the middle watch. We ride at dawn. Now turn in and get some sleep.'

'Yes Sire.' I said as I rose and went to piss on a tree.

'For tomorrow, there will be blood, and more blood.' Quoted Wilf,

'It always happens that way.'

As I stared in to the night, I thought of how my destiny was now tied to this Warlord and what a strange man, for truth, he was. As I contemplated I realised that none of us really knew anything about him at all. To some eyes the Warlord was a peculiar man; silent and brooding. He definitely has a temper on him; as sharp as his sword's edge. He has a penetrating eye too; it goes with his lazy half smile. Yet, at times, he can be open and even friendly; willing to listen to the suggestions of his men. And still, some how, he doesn't seem to fit in to the world of High Österriech. He has a peculiar habit of shivering whenever he looked up at the snow-topped mountains that sit huddled in the distant east. He looks like a man who has gazed upon the Halls of Hell and knows that, one day soon, he will be heading that way again.

He is a tall and muscular man with shoulder length dirty blond hair which is now fading to grey at the temples. He wears a heavy beard but keeps his neck clean shaved. He stands about six and a half feet tall and moves as swiftly as a cat. Still; the one single thing thing that everyone notices about him is his deep blue eyes with their strange epicedian fold.

He carries a double headed axe which he calls 'Swift' and that is never far from his reach and has a curved sabre, the 'Empress's Kiss', which is covered in some strange types of runes. That blade had a cruel curve near the centre of its percussion, but closer to the tip, and it is as deadly in the cut and slash of a cavalry charge as it was in the thrust and stab of close combat.

I has been the Warlord's soldier now for five months and that was as long as anyone of the Komrades. I had learned that no one at the castle had been with him for more than eight months. Not the kitchen girls; nor even the stable lads. And the gossip in the castle said that the Lord's woman and his child, Yuri, had both died of the same yellow fever that killed my brother Ditmar; and which the Gods had spread through the lands five or more years ago. Maybe that is what had made him such a solitary man? Or was it the pressure of command? There is no doubt that he was determined man. One who had a purpose in life; a purpose that the rest of us could only guess at. That maybe the reason that the King had chosen him to foster the Prince? Still…I had heard it whispered quietly in the shadows;

'That death kept company with him…as the moon and stars accompany the Goddess Nyx.'

I stamped my feet to keep them warm and watched the still night. Guard duty is always lonely. My mind drifted to Freya again; wet and squealing with pleasure, her juices seeping down my shaft, as she bounced up and down on my cock and I felt a half stiffy growing in my breeches.

It was turning cold now. The dark was coming on, and I could smell that the rain was about to start again. I listen to the night and rubbed my hands together; wishing and waiting for my watch to end and longing for my bed roll.

The next night we stayed at the Priory of Saint Florian which sits on the outskirts of the city of Linz. We ate the same sparse food as the monks. I sat with little Prince Rudolf, and Sir Johannus. Further down the same table sat Wilf and Dagmar. They were playing dice with Steinmann. He was a mean, ill-tempered lout from Bavaria. A natural born killer if ever there was one. He grumbled about everything. Unusually; tonight he seemed happy for once. We were heading towards his homelands. The Komrades were taking bets on how long it would be before he deserted or was hanged.

The Warlord sat at a low table removed from the rest of us. His only companion was a small, strange, and unidentified Priest. The Priest was also staying at the priory for the night and taking his rest from his own travels.

We all ate the same simple mutton stew with large pieces of stone ground bread followed by ripe pears and a soft cheese. We drank the monks own brew: a light bier with a bittersweet taste. I watched the Warlord and the Priest as they ate; their heads inclined together. Their conversation was far too low to be overheard. And as hard as we tried none of us was able to discern what was being said at that table. They talked for a long time. After the meal was concluded they rose and walked the length of the hall. As they passed down the hall the Priest was heard to say.

'…We will be ready to move when we hear from you. Your messenger should deliver this ring to me.' The Priest took the ring from his finger and passing it over to the Warlord.

'When he delivers this; I will understand from

whom he has come. Do not use the couriers nor an envoy. The networks are polluted…and their spies will be monitoring them.'

The Warlord reached out and took the ring and placed it in a pocket; deep within his robes.

'You will need to be cautious. That Eunuch has his spies everywhere. And the Inquisition is penetrating ever further across Germania. Between them; they have infiltrated the whole palace. I strongly believe that the spineless Volker and that damned Eunuch are plotting a move. This King is addled by his eighty and four years. And he is too slow to die. And yet… the young Prince, Otto…He died so quickly. Some think it was unnaturally quickly…'

The pair passed out of the refectory and on to the terrace. Outside they walked slowly towards the wooden bridge that crossed the water garden. Here they paused looking down at the duckweed and sweet flag that floated on the ponds surface and their conversation was lower still; even though they couldn't be overheard. The night drew in around them and the stars started to appear in the evening sky before they bowed their heads to each other and went their separate ways.

6

The Ancient and Holy City of Munich

Milo Bauermann; is in the retinue of the Warlord and has been designated to protect the young Prince Rudolf, who is dressed as a page. They are leaving the Priory of Saint Florian and heading west again.

The next morning the Priory echoed with the sound of the tertiary stable boys as they rushed about their duties. The horses snorted and stamped; eager to be off. The men were quickly swallowing the last of their morning beer and complaining; like all soldiers do. They were cursing, as was usual, about having to rise with the dawn. We readied for the journey and mounted our horses in the courtyard. The early morning sunlight streamed weakly over the outer buildings and the smell in the air was of more rain to come.

The Warlord was seated on his huge black stallion. Ackus was a reckless, ill-tempered beast; more willingly to bite you than it would bite an apple. The Warlord shaded his eyes and nodded at old Sir Johannus, who snorted roughly and then spat out a mouth full of snot. He barked the order to mount and make ready to move.

'Come on you lazy shits, let's be having you ready,

mount up. We are leaving. Anyone who is late will be fined half a day's pay.'

The Warlord spurred his great black stallion in to a leap and rode out through the open gate. We followed; riding in pairs. I rode with the Prince who looked tired and drawn as if a cold was beginning to set in.

We eased our pace as we approached the crest of a hill. It was the early afternoon. Five days since we had left Linz. We reined in and stopped in a place where the road twisted around a cluster of, wind swept, bent back trees. They marked the way to the city. Soon we had started the long, slow, winding descent towards the city that sprawled across the valley floor.

The Ancient and Holy City of Munich was built to be exactly ten square leagues across and it took a grid formation. It reflect the rectangular shape of the world. We surveyed the sight as the afternoon sun glistened on the towers of the Luminous Palace. The golden roof of the Holy Temple of Virtue, which they say is made of solid gold, shone brightly.

The river Isar cut the city at an angle and meanders in a lazy fashion out towards the eastern gate. As I rode forward with the Prince I heard the comment;

'This is where we will enter.'

The Warlord was speaking; recognising the weak point in the cities defences and indicating with his finger to Sir Johannus.

'So few Lord? My Lord, so few as we are…cannot expect to take the Ancient and Holy City of Munich.' Said Old Johannus nervously.

It was the the first time I had heard doubt in his voice.

'There are more ways of taking a city than storming its walls.' Retorted the Warlord.

'Being so few…I hope we have not been recognised

as a threat by the emperor's spies. We will keep our formation and simply ride in through the gate. Pass the word to the men. They should keep silent. Their weapons must be concealed…but ready.'

Our column approached the eastern gate at a steady pace. Not fast enough to be threatening to the guards and still not indicating that we were preparing to slow down. The City Guards ran out in front of the gate. They occupied the area between the City Wall and the bridge that crossed over the river. They formed up into two ranks and presented their spears; grounding the bases against a charge.

The Sentinel in his high tower sent a flare high into the sky. It spluttered and shot out bright red sparks in a large ark across the city. The gates behind the guards swung closed with a heavy resounding bang. That sound was followed closely by a dull thud as the bar was dropped and we heard the noise of men struggling with heavy weights as the wooded braces were put in place across the back of those so solid gates.

After we had crossed the bridge Sir Johannus raised his hand and we eased to a gentle halt. We formed a line of mounted death; just a few paces in front of the guards. Our horses snorted and stamped; ready to leap into a charge. The Warlord guided his mount forward until he was only a stride away from the guards.

The Captain of the Guard advanced and with a firm manor and demanded;

'Declare yourself!'

'You know who I am.' Snarled the Warlord.

'Why do you enter the Ancient and Holy City of Munich without being announced and so…escorted by an armed force?' Demanded the Captain of the Guard.

'I come to pay my respects to the King.' Replied the

Warlord.

'Would you have me travel unprotected in such an unsettled time?'

The Captain looked about and demanded;

'You will wait here until the Watch Commander arrives.'

'You would dare to keep one of the King's Councillors waiting?' Screamed the Warlord.

The Captain shrank visibly under the onslaught and many of the guard were seen to take a backward step.

'These…these are my orders…My Lord.'

The Captain swallowed hard and hoped he would still be a captain when the sun went down. Fortunately for him and before any further escalation could take place, the Watch Commander arrived and shouted from the wall above the gate. The Guard snapped to attention and the Captain rushed to the walls to speak with him. After the briefest of conversations, and a short pause, one of the gates was again opened and the commander appeared before us. He was mounted on a brown mare.

He advanced to the Warlord and bowing his head very deeply he removed his gauntlet and held it in his left hand lazily. He tugged at his left ear with his right hand. Then he scratched his nose before tugging on the right ear. All the time watching the Warlord.

'Please excuse our Captain. He is only following his orders. We are at a high security level. Everyone… with out exception is being held at the gates.'

He paused and edged his horse forward a few steps and lowering his voice, spoke softly so that only those close by could hear.

'I am Sir Lother, My Lord. Please forgive my tardiness…and this reception. We did not expect you so soon. Please be assured that no disrespect is meant.

For I too search for the Lost Symbol.' He continued after a moment.

'Please…let me escort you. Do you desire to see the Chamber of Reflection?'

'Why is the security so high?'

The Warlord lazily scratched his nose with his left hand and then patted his chest before checking that his sword was still loose.

'Because the King has insisted.' Sir Lother replied simply with a wave of his hand.

'However we will be please to allow you to pass. Unfortunately, you will only be able to bring a small bodyguard of two men with you. The rest of your men can stay at the barracks or find rooms in the outer city…back across the river.'

'No bodyguard will be necessary.' The Warlord turned on his horse and shouted his orders to Sir Johannus. We wheeled our horses and rode proudly back over the bridge. We would find some lodgings in the outer city. I watched as the Warlord spurred his horse and headed through the now open gates. The Watch Commander rode swiftly after him.

7

The Warlord's Message

The Warlord; is in the Great and Holy City of Munich awaiting his meetings with King Henry, called the Lion of Bavaria. And with the High Priest.

I could still smell the fear; a heavy deep sweat that clung to the Commander even though Sir Lother had declared himself to me. I gentled Ackus as the Commander led us through the streets. We rode deep into the city. Eventually to the Inner Courtyard of the Lower Bailey. Here several eunuchs waited to show me to an apartment that was kept in readiness for guests and where I was to await for the call from the King.

Sir Lother was a slight man. He had too many teeth for his small, thin-lipped mouth. He chatted inanely as we rode through the city. He answered his own questions; like some men who think of themselves as important often do.

'…How where the roads? Muddy eh? Always are… this time of year…still, I hear there has been a good crop and the harvest will begin in a week or so…the rain should hold off, don't you think? Yes, I'm sure it will. Did you encounter any trouble journeying? No, not with your excellent troops…I can tell a good squad of men when I see them. The Priest told me to watch out for you. Good man that Priest. Have you know him long? No I suppose not. He is a secretive man and new in the kings service…and you have been…travelling. No? Yes, I know of your travels… Who has not? So few have been to the Far East. And so I made sure I had the Watch Command. Of course, it's not my usual duty…no indeed; for I am high in the King's favour…and the Bishop's too…'

Once inside the apartments I removed my armour and washed my hands and face; before changing my chemise. And then sitting at the scribing desk I took a quill and stroked the feather down my cheek as I thought. Slowly I dipped it in the dark black ink and then quickly scratched it across the parchment. I wrote a note in my best hand. The note read simply:

> *'Your Holiness, I am here in the city ~*
> *to pay homage to the King.*
> *I must leave as soon as my audience*
> *is over; to continue my King's work*
> *~ the search for the Lost Symbol.*
> *But I would crave an interview with*
> *you.*
>
> *~ LB ~*

I carefully scraped my signature across the bottom of the parchment and warmed the small wax stick over the flame of the candle. Then I watched as it dripped on to the paper. It formed a dark, midnight black pool on the fold and I placing the ring that the Priest had given me into the wax. I pressed down hard with a satisfying smile. It made a clean impression. And so the note was sealed with the symbol of a snake coiled around a skull.

'Sometimes the old ways serve us better.' I said to myself as I placed the note on a tray and rang a small silver bell that was sitting silently on the scribing desk.

The servant left the apartment to deliver the note; and I knew he would take it directly to the Head Eunuch.

8

The Secret Plan of the Head Eunuch

Matilda of England; the Anointed Holy Roman Empress, the Queen of the Romans, Queen of Bavaria, Duchess of Saxony, and the daughter of a King, the sister of Kings, and of Dukes; from across the world and the true Queen of England, and all its empire; is closeted in her solar with the Head Eunuch and Volker, the Chancellor.

The Head Eunuch eased an extremely sharp, thin bladed, dagger between the wax seal and the parchment. Using all his skills he carefully prised them apart. He read the letter carefully. He read it again before handing it to Volker, the King's Chancellor and advisor.

I tapped my foot on the floor and scowled. I waited for the letter to be passed to me. Between us we ruled the Ten Kingdoms and held the fifty and eight little Principalities in the palm of our collective hand. It had taken me years to gain this control and I intended to keep it! As long as I could manipulate every aspect of the life of King Henry, the Lion of Bavaria, my old and now infirm husband. And the more power I had; the more power I realised that I could take. For these men were such fools. Weak and self-serving. Oh, why was I born a woman in a man's world?

'Do we search for something that is not there? Has he brought the Prince, my son, with him? What King's work? What lost symbol?' I asked my fellow conspirators.

'It maybe a secret communication. A code.' Replied the Chancellor.

'The Warlord and this new Priest are up to something.' I said to the Head Eunuch.

'Yes; but what can one man do?' The Chancellor questioned the air.

'I would like to kill them both.' I said and crunched up the parchment between my delicate fingers.

'That would be a dangerous thing to do, Your Grace. And without the Prince in our possession. Not within our power...'

'Dare we. It would not be easy to achieve such a thing?' Replied the Chancellor.

'Yes. But if it could be achieved...' I paused.

'Come on boys...take the bait!' I thought to myself.

My poor mothers heart was pounding at the thought of seeing my son again. It had been five years since the King had decided to foster him. And he a child barely old enough to walk. And against all my wishes and all my pleas.

He had arranged for him to be with his cousin Frederick, the Duke of Swabia but then they had a falling out and instead the High Priest had recommended this Warlord. The Warlord had recently found high favour by his might and his fiercely won battles in the King's name.

The court had known very little of this Warlord but I remembered him. And so when the yellow fever had spread across the kingdom ~ killing hundreds every day ~ it was swiftly decided that Rudolf would be far safer away from the disease. He was taken to the Warlord's castle in the mountains of High Österriech.

Rudolf had less than two years when they prised him from my bosom. What a small boy he had been. He had soft, dark hair that curled around his ears. I had seen him only twice since then and in fairness he had grown well and his hair had come in darker; almost a black and he had lost those lovely curls.

'Surely, if we hold the Warlord, then I'm confident you could manipulate the position to one were by the Prince would be delivered safely to the King… and so in turn to us.' I told them.

'If we let these conspirators meet…encouraged them to meet. A secret meeting. A meeting upon which we can spy and then…' I let the sentence hang.

'It is time for you two clowns to perform your own parts in this little play.'

'We can have the palace guards arrest them!' Finished the Head Eunuch.

'We would then have our proof…and can accuse them of treason. Accuse them of planning an uprising against the King!' Replied the Chancellor.

'It is a daring plan. I'm not sure we should…' I said letting the tension hang in the air. Palpable. Teasing.

'…But would we be believed? The high Priest is a powerful man?' I asked. Nudging the plan along. Slowly ~ like icing sugar spelling out the name on a feast day cake.

'Jesu! You stupid weak men! Must I lead you by the hand?'

'And the Warlord is a dangerous and a deadly one.' I concluded.

'Yes, I agree. But, we can plant the evidence in the Warlord's apartments. Plant it after he leaves for the meeting. We would have unassailable proof that they are both traitors. And thus would use the same arrow to kill both birds.' The Head Eunuch finished.

'Daring…brilliantly so, Your Grace.' Said the Chan-

cellor wringing his hands like some demon in a
street theatre production.

Sometimes I was bewildered by these two. How on
earth had they ever managed to get themselves into
a position where they could control the King? I mean
to say. They were stupid men. Weak idiots. Well
not stupid…no, they were clever-ish; in that mean,
common, street life sort of way. But not the brilliant
minds that I would need once I had the power.

'What can we loose if they confront us? After all…
we have the best interests of our King at heart. We
carry out only his wishes.' I told them slyly.

They both smiled and took some wine that a slave
offered from the tray he held above is head as he
knelt before us. I nodded;

'And I was never here…' I thought.

'So be it. Here's to their meeting.' I said.

The Eunuch gently raised his glass and touched it
to that of the Chancellors and mine.

9

Death of a King

Matilda of England; the Anointed Holy Roman Empress, the Queen of the Romans, Queen of Bavaria, Duchess of Saxony, and the daughter of a King, the sister of Kings, and of Dukes; from across the world and the true Queen of England, and all its empire; is close with her husband, Henry, the Lion of Bavaria, in his bed chamber.

Also present, as custom demands, are Henry's advisors: the High Eunuch, Chancellor Volker, Docktor Schabel Von Rom his medic, and a Priest.

The King lay in his bed. The pillows were piled high and his head laid back against them. The pillows in turn rested on the elaborate headrest of carved oak upon which was adorned the crest of the family of Welf: The Dukes of Saxony. It was deeply carved and covered in gold leaf; a Unicorn with a crown on the one side and a rampant lion, dexter, to the other.

He looked all of his eighty and four years. His bald head was covered liberally with dark liver spots. His face was framed by long grey side-whiskers that were matted with the grease and the sweat that poured from his brow. His hands shook with a slight tremor and his lizard like tongue slithered slowly over his dry lips.

I felt my loathing for him oozing up from my very bones. Here lay the awful man that I had been betrothed to at the age of eight. Married to by twelve; still only a girl…for Jesu' sake. And me a royal child too. I was the grand daughter of the Conqueror!

And he had robbed me of my best years…sucked them dry. Like a piglet sucking on a sow. And he had failed me too. Failed me as a man and failed me as a lover. Failed as a father too. And in his duties as a husband; being already old and ailing when we married. Oh, that was no wedding night. He had struggled to rise to the occasion. Then, and on every opportunity since!

Rudolph had been an indiscretion…after all I am a young woman still. And my husband was far too arrogant to suspect that the child may not be his own. But I dare not repeat the process. That would be a step too far. Yes. He was stupid enough, and arrogant enough to not suspect but worse! He didn't even care. He did not care that I had no other children. He had a brood already from his first wife; Clementia. She had given him a host of frail girls and weak boys including his heir; Otto of Bavaria, who had died of a sudden illness six moons ago.

I replaced my husband's medics annually. I had done for five years now but still he had steadfastly refused to die.

I bowed low before him. Closed my eyes and kissed him lightly on his forehead. Then I looked in to his weak blue eyes. There remained the last sparkle of energy. The remnants of his spirit. It flickered slightly and shone for a moment. As once, long ago, had he.

'I will wish you a pleasant nights sleep, Your Grace.' I said and as I bowed again before I left the room.

'Yes, Yes…damn you woman, Jesu…stop you're

fussin'. Leave me be! Leave me…will you?' The King waved a liver spotted hand.

Volker and the High Eunuch remained with his medic, Schnabel von Rom, and the funny little Priest. They all bowed their heads to me in turn as I departed. My eyes caught Volker's and they flashed at him ~ like a woman's eyes do when they play with the soul of a man.

The High Eunuch cleared his throat and addressing the King he began the nightly ritual. He and Volker would deliver their tedious reports and the medic would fuss, tut, and pamper, as he wiped the drool from the side of the King's mouth. And all the while the Priest would be delivering Vespers in a soft whisper. Although no-one in particular would take an moments notice of him or his prayers.

As the chamber door closed behind me I could hear Volker droning on about taxes and crop yields…and the complaints of one of the smaller principalities.

'…Your Grace…and the Prince of Grafschaft Bentheim has raised a complaint about infringements… within his borders…against the Bishopric of Munster.'

'Jesu, the Gods damn all bishops.' Said Henry as he lay back on his pillows.

'Tell the Prince, what ever his name is…?'

'…Prince Ludwig, Highness.' Replied Volker.

'…Another one? Jesu! Tell this Ludwig…that we shall send a stern message to the Bishop of Muster… ordering him to desist these…infringements immediately…and we will award the usual compensation…upon your report Volker.'

'Yes Highness. And the Bishop?'

'We will make him pay. Fine him…Jesu damn all Bishops! Five thousands silver shillings…they hate it when you attack their purse…better allow payment in goods, if he so desires, and he will! The snivelling little shit…and send a letter to the Pope, saying; If he can not control his Bishops…then I will!'

'Is that wise Your Grace? We have only just repaired relations with the Pope's church. And they will claim that the Bishop is not subject to our Salic laws…but to their own Canon laws.'

'Damn the Pope. He is just a French puppet. Damn him and the bishops too. You're a Bishop are you not?' He asked the Priest.

'No, Your Grace. Just a lowly Priest. How may I be of service?'

Henry paused to get his breath and looked at the man for the first time. He screwed up his nose as if the Priest was permeating a stench that was nauseating. Then after a moment he continued.

'Tell that Pope of yours…' He breathed deeply for a moment,

'…tell him that if he ever dare come north, he will get a warm welcome…like the fires of hell, Jesu!' He coughed violently.

'Damn all Priests…Von Rom where is my draft?'

The medic had prepared the King's night potion. He did this every night. He approached the King's bed. And, as he stepped up, Volker indicated to Schnabel to pass it over to him. Volker performed an obsequious bow with an exaggerated flourish of his hand and he held the small glass forward for the King.

'Allow me, Your Grace.'

The King took his drink in his shaking hand and tossed it down in one quick deliberate action, as was his way. Volker withdrew taking the empty glass and holding it behind his back.

Within a brief moment a terrible, violent spasm shook Henry's body. He cried out. And no sound came. Only blood. A deep, thick, dark red blood slowly oozed from between his lips and began to dribble from the corner of his mouth. He began to choke. He gasp for air as he struggled to breathe. And then he croaked pitifully.

'You…sly…little man.' He whispered, pointing a shaking finger at Volker. Volker stared about wide-eyed. The High Eunuch gasped.

The King's death cry was not loud. No not loud ~ yet it seemed to echo through the palace; as it would later echo through the whole of Germania. And as he died his eyes lost what little sparkle remained and his blackened tongue twisted manically to the side of his mouth.

The Warlord with the King's Guards, led by Sir Lother, rushed into the room surrounding the High Eunuch, Volker, and Doctor Schnabel von Rom. As the Priest moved to meet them he suddenly seemed to grow in stature. Taller. His back straightened. His old man gait became more spritely, as if he had suddenly become ten years younger, and I realised that I had never really paid him any attention at all!

'A trio ordré. How splendid!'

I had to remember not to laugh out loud.

'Interesting. Someone else is in this game. And they have made the first move. But who in the name of the Gods is this Priest? And how has he taken control of the situation?'

I winked a bit of dust from my eyelash as I quietly replaced the notch in the hollowed-out curve of the wall. The hollow fit my face so well. Almost as if it had been made for me. The well-greased notch slid back across the bolt head of the candle stanchion without a sound. I shook myself free of dust and smoothed down and straightened my dress. Then I made my way through the darkness. I kept my hand out, feeling the roughly chiselled stonework, as I went. Silently counting the notches that were raised there; every second stride.

'Eins, zwei, drei…'

And then I was at the corner of the wall. Here a small candle was placed in a niche. And there, just a few paces to the left, I found the stone steps that led downwards and twisted through the tunnel-like spaces that led back to my rooms. Once there I disrobed and lay quietly on the bed. I would wait for the guards to bring me the sad news of the murder of my poor husband. Poor Henry…Henry the Lion, The King of Bavaria, Duke of Saxony et alia. And as I lay there I reach down and plucking a grape began to suck softly. I smiled as I thought about the plans I would instigate now that I was the Queen, and Regent in my son Rudolf's name.

'First, I will arrange for Rudolf to be brought to the palace. Immediately. And ensure that he is kept safe. Then…then, there would be the Warlord and this Priest to deal with. Rewards, and then an accident or two, I think.' I said to Dark Prussia as she lay snuggling with pleasure on my bed. I fed her a grape too.

'Although this Warlord…he is not bad to look at. He may make me a good husband. A battle hardened warrior, and a killer, if ever there was one…Yes, he is a man to know. And we will need a new High Priest too…there is plenty of time for Rudolf to develop…' I smiled.

Dark Prussia said nothing. Those deep green eyes of her's smiled also. She turned her nose up at the grape and instead stretched out her long legs, entwining them with mine and placed her head on my breast. I felt her as she slipped inside my rob and she scratched playfully at the low hairs that spread upwards on to my soft, smooth stomach.

10

The Great Emperor

Milo Bauermann; and his Komrades have been included in the 'Honour'; the advance column of the Imperial Guard who would accompany the Prince to his coronation. All the nobles of the land are assembled for the ceremony.

'Honour Guard…Mount!' Came Sir Lother's command. The day before yesterday the Warlord had gathered us in the small courtyard off the eastern tower and Sir Johannus had drill us for two hours. It had been hot and thirsty work. Dagmar and Steinmann, who the men called Stig, had done nothing but complain but they did not complain too loudly.

Then Old Johannus had us line up for inspection parade. The Warlord walked up and down the ranks. He stopped to adjust a fastening here and check a blade for rust - my own as it happens - and then he stood in front of us and spoke softly.

'Men…there are some momentous times a head of us. Dangerous times. Some of us will die!'

We looked at each other through the corner of our eyes as he continued.

'It is time for you to choose. You can fight for me or you can fight against me. Choose now and none will be disgraced…thought less of…or harmed in any fashion. If you wish to leave…Sir Johannus will have your monies drawn and ready for you by noon.'

'Some of us will die soon and some will have great rewards. I want you all, if you have the lettering, to make a declaration. Name who you would like monies and wages to be paid to if you do not survive. If you don't have the lettering, Prester John and the Priest have offered to write for you. And for those that would depart. Now is the hour.'

We all looked around and slowly our eyes descended on Stig. He had made no secret of his wish to go home and now we were in Munich; he was but a few days ride away. Stig put his head down and shuffled his feet; avoiding all eye contact.

'Good…Sir Johannus has judged you well. In that case you will find a barrel of wine back at your lodgings. Drink deep…for tomorrow you shall all become Kingsmen. You will be enrolled as the Honour Guard! Sworn to protect the King with your life. You will continue under my personal leadership. We shall soon be seeing action.'

'Battle, Blood, and Booty!' He declared.

'Battle, Blood, and Booty!' We chanted in reply and raised our swords high. We shouted it again and again.

✪

The 'Honour' of the Imperial Guard rode at the head of the column escorting the procession. We were led jointly by Sir Lother and Sir Johannus. Immediately to our rear was the young Prince. He was seated on a pure white Arabian stallion. It moved with a steady confident stride and riding easily behind him was the Warlord on Ackus.

The Warlords appearance had caused some comments; none of us had ever seen him clean-shaven before. It was a definite improvement. And for the first time he looked content with his lot in life. He also looked ten or more years younger than I had first estimated.

A buzz grew in the crowd as we passed by and one or two people in the crowd whispered to their neighbour; a name from the past. And soon it spread, softly spoken and with a hint of fear.

'Louis...'

✪

A huge gong shimmered and the sound sailed through out the room as the mutes opened the large, ornate wooden doors. They turned and bowed before the procession and the many acolytes now began chanting. Their heads were totally shaven. Bald; apart from the slim strip of short-cropped hair that ran in a thin band from the forehead back towards the crown.

'That's a good place for flies to land.' I had joked in a whispered aside to Wilf. His eyes smiled but Sir Johannus looked daggers at me and harrumphed an expletive that meant;

'Silence you fool!'

As we progressed a strong smell of incense began to fill the air. The long argent flags, trimmed in sable, stirred in the breeze. They hung from the ceiling. They were emblazoned with a double-headed eagle; Sable on a field of Gules.

The columns of Priests moved slowly through the city. They came through the south gate. They moved with a purpose. They progressed toward the Holy Temple of Virtue. Once inside they moved up to the High Alter.

As the procession entered the Temple the Priests filtered away from us and the 'Honour' formed into single lines. We moved down each side of the inner chamber.

All the nobles of the country surged towards the tables. They pushed and shoved each other with their elbows. Determined to be closest to the action. We held firm and eventually everyone was seated to the plan that had been displayed. It had been carefully worked out by the High Priest and implemented by his acolytes. Soon order was installed and the ceremony continued.

The young Prince, who was now dismounted, moved easily to the centre of the alter. The Warlord followed close behind. Now the chanting stopped. The gong clashed again. As it reverberated through the hall the new High Priest, the Priest we had seen at the Priory of Saint Florian, bowed to the young Prince and turned to address the crowd.

'Noble Lords. Grand Council of Germania.' His voice was crisp and clear.

'We are gathered here…after the sad death of Henry the Lion, King of Bavaria, Duke of Saxony.' He paused and took his time to glance around the room.

'It is my duty…as your High Priest…to anoint a new King to reign over the Ten Kingdoms of High Österriech. To protect the Kingdom's, the Principality states…and all the people of the realms there in.'

He studied the hall.

'We will create a new realm. A new realm for a new King!'

'Germania!' He emphasised loudly.

'We must defeat our enemies!'

'We must defeat our enemies!' We chanted in unison, stamping our right foot loudly ~ just as we had been practicing all week.

Now more quietly;

'I have prayed to the Gods…and to the spirits of the four winds.' The High Priest continued in his slight foreign brogue.

'To the sun and the moon. I have consulted all the wise men of the kingdom…and the Holy Monks in their mountain retreat.' He paused again for effect.

'I have read the will of the High One…and I have consulted with the Royal Astrologist. The omnipotent signs are clearly identifiable. The Gods have spoken to me…and I deliver their commands.' Another pause.

'The Prince, Otto, heir of the late King is dead… these six moons now.' Then in a quieter, more gentler tone, the former Priest continued.

'The chosen one is not the eldest surviving male of the old King's children…who alas the Gods have declared to be weak…and deemed unfit for the office. But…he is the eldest son of the late King by his mighty Queen…Queen Matilda of England, the Anointed Holy Roman Empress, the Queen of the Romans, the Queen of Bavaria, the Duchess of Saxony, and the daughter of a King, the sister of Kings, and of Dukes…all across the world, and the true Queen of England and all its Empire.'

We cheered.

'He will soon come to full manhood. He is strong. He is healthy. He is young. And he is of Munich!'

He waited for the cheering to die down again.

'And with the guidance of the Grand Council…he will be the wisest of his dynasty. The greatest King yet! An Emperor of Germania!'

A huge roar erupted from the crowd.

The High Priest continued as he took the crown from the cushion upon which it rested. He held it high…and then moved it ritually through the four Stations of the Cross before he turned towards the young boy who knelt in front of him. He paused and looked about the hall. Slowly he placed the crown on the young boys head. Then with the same ritual he took the Sword of the Nation and placed this in the young man's hands.

Trumpets blared and the assemble crowd cheered. The eldest councillor approach and bowed as he offer to the Emperor the 'Book of Wisdom' and a small, leather pouch full of golden coins.

'The book is to help the King rule wisely…and the gold; so that he will not be corrupt. I give you the new King and your Emperor!' Announced the High Priest.

There was an almighty cheer from everyone and the trumpets blared as they reverberated around the hall again.

'The Holy Emperor, Rudolf the First.' We stamped our feet down again; repeating the chant.

'Rudolf the First!'

'King of Bavaria…King of the Romans…Duke of Saxony…ruler of all Germania…from the jewel of our Ancient and Holy City of Munich to the lofty mountains of High Österriech, from the great rivers Rhine and Danube to the vast Northern seas. And through his mother…the rightful King of England and all her Empire.'

'The Great Emperor!' We all chanted.

'The Great Emperor!'

'The Great Emperor!'

All the assembly bowed down to their new ruler and there arose an ecstatic cheering as again the huge gong shimmered through the hall. As the noise faded away the High Priest spoke out again but this time his voice held a definite menace.

'Let those who are not obedient… Leave our city now!'

11

The Great Hall of the Luminous Palace.

Milo Bauermann; has been appointed to the 'Honour', the elite of the Imperial Guard, who protect the Great Emperor with their very lives.

All the nobles of the land are assembled in Munich. They are progressing from the Holy Temple of Virtue to the Great Hall of the Luminous Palace for the celebration feast of the coronation .

The Great Emperor led the procession back through the Holy Temple of Virtue and across the city park. The park is world renown for its magnificent dancing water fountains. The procession made it way into the Great Hall of the Luminous Palace.

The Great Hall was lit by hundreds of torches and candles. It was festooned with decorations and blooming with flowers. The long argent flags draped from the high ceiling to the brilliantly patterned marble floor. Each with a huge double headed, sable eagle sitting upon a field of gules. The new symbol of the Holy Empire of Germania.

It seemed as if the noble people of the whole country were assembled in the banqueting hall. Their tables were stretched out in long rows which led-off from the high table, which sat raised by a dais, and they ran across the top of the room. They ran underneath a carved and gilded display of the world with the newly formed Germania in its centre and the ice rim at its edge.

Spirited, rhythmic, music came floating down from the gallery high above, and I recognised it as Wagner's Valkyrie. The city of Vienna was famous for its dancers. They came from as far as India and the Great Russia's to be trained in the famous dance schools. A troop had been sent especially for the ceremony and the beautiful, half naked, dancers performed in the area in front of the dais and more wove in and out between the rows of tables.

The banquet was laid out in front of the emperor and the food was more than plentiful. A continuous procession of dishes. Spicy soup, pheasant, and grouse. Rabbit, oysters, salmon, and sea trout. Roasted cranes, and suckling pigs. Wild boar and venison. Two whole roast oxen turned on the massive spits that stood in front of the fireplaces at each the side of the room. They were continuously basted by the ladle boys, who operated a chained system of cogs, as the marinaded the meat with spiced red wine from the Mediterranean sea states.

The highlight of the feast arrived to a blaze of trumpets and an almighty cheer. A cheer that rolled down the hall in a wave as the procession of serving girls passed holding their trays high.

Two dozen, black, double necked swans, presented so that they resembled the new Germanic symbol and sitting on a lake of gold and red.

And all through the day the drink flowed freely and everyone helped themselves generously; the nobles indulged liberally in the feast.

I stood with my back to the wall. I could hear my stomach rumbling ~ it must have thought my throat had been cut ~ as the smell of the roast oxen permutate the air.

The Emperor sat in the centre of the high table with the Warlord at his right and the Queen Regent at his left. Next to his mother sat the High Priest. Their entrance together had caused a massive buzz of excitement; tinged with a slightly subdued edge of apprehension.

Now I was close to the new High Priest and for the first time I could see him properly. I immediately recognised him from the Priory of Saint Florian. He was a small stocky man who spoke with a Scottish lilt to his voice. His hair was receding across his balding head. He had a sharp chiselled face that was completely dominated by savage hooked nose and big sad, pale blue eyes.

The Queen regent was chatting happily to him. I overheard her saying that she was:

'… simply ecstatic to have my son restored to me after the long, lonely years. You know he was not more than eighteen moons, maybe twenty, when his father had insisted, against all my pleads, to have him fostered. I know it was to spare him from the yellow fever but a mother….well she misses her only son. It is only natural…I must say that I'm simply amazed by how much he has grown. He has become such a strong, fine boy. It's simply miraculous, and he has grown into a young warrior…it must be all that fresh mountain air. And to think he was such a sickly looking child; Weren't you Rudolf? You always seemed to have a cold in the head and a sore, red nose from the sniffles.'

She held the young Emperor close; pushing him deep into her ample breasts, like a mother does. The young man reddened slightly.

'Mother… please.'

Queen Matilda was happy. She laughed as she released him.

'Boys, eh?'

'I really don't know what you have been feeding him, My Lord Louis!' She said turning to the Warlord.

He smiled at her and looked embarrassed.

'Just the normal stuff, Your Grace. He has a fine appetite.'

The Emperor's half brothers and half sisters, cousins, and cousins once, and twice removed…indeed all the family relations were spread among the other important guests at the central outer tables. They had been raise above the inner tables and stretched on either side down the length of the hall. However it was not customary nor was it seen fit for the older women, those past child bearing age, of the royal family to be permitted to attend the feast. The nature of such occasions was far too bawdy. They had their own separate feast in the smaller, 'Ehefrau Halle' of the palace.

I watched Rudolf, the new Emperor, as he sat at the high table. He ate sparsely. Indeed it was rumoured that he had eat privately before the feast.

He sat there, almost in a daze, and snatched swift glances at Duke Louis, the Warlord, as if he was seeing him for the first time ~ now he was without a beard; he was unrecognisable.

The High Emperor looked distracted, somewhat dazed, and overwhelmed by the occasion. And who could really blame him. It had been quite a day for the young man. He stared blankly around the room, picking occasionally at his plate, and sometimes taking a small sip from his glass.

The noise in the hall was terrific. It sounded as if everyone was talking at the same time but as if no one was actually saying anything. And the High Emperor looked as if he were a player, sat upon the stage, in some strange play. A play that was being performed all around him. And indeed he may have been.

As the feast progressed many of the nobles, seeking to ingratiate themselves with the new High Emperor, had made very flattering, flowery, and interminable speeches.

The Warlord would be the last speaker. And eventually the time came. He rose and waited for silence. Slowly the room fell quiet and here and there the name 'Louis' was whispered again in disbelief.

The Warlord looked to the new High Emperor and then to the Queen Regent and he smiled. The High Emperor acknowledged the smile with his eyes as he took another small drink. The Queen looked impassive and beautiful, she smiled to herself. A proud mother basking in the reflected glory.

The Warlords eyes darted to the High Priest and an unspoken knowledge passed between them. The Warlord stood respectfully and he began to speak slowly but with meaning and purpose. He praised the late King, and then spoke of the Great Emperor's strengths.

'...I have watched His Imperial Majesty grow from a small child in to a fine boy...and watch that boy become a splendid young man. And...I believe that with the Queen Regents help, the Great Emperor will be the strongest, the wisest, and the bravest of all... The Great Emperor!'

The crowds knew a cue when they heard one. They stood to a man, cheering and shouting.

'The Great Emperor!'

'The Great Emperor!'

The toast echoed off the roof. The Warlord looked around the hall before he continued:

'I will live and die for my Emperor. And I will destroy all my Emperors enemies.'

And at this moment he raised a glass of wine and

said;

'Your Imperial Majesty, Your Grace, My Lords, and all the noble folk of Germania. I give you a toast. Long live the Great Emperor…long may he reign…in health and in peace.'

'The Great Emperor!'

The assemble guests rose again and drank with him.

'The Great Emperor!'

'The Great Emperor!'

'The Great Emperor!'

As one ~ we of the Imperial Guards ~ moved silently from our designated locations along the wall and stood close behind the guests.

I placed my un-gloved hand over the girl's mouth, twisting her head towards me. I looked into her startled dark eyes. My knife slid across her throat easily. It flashing brightly in the candle light. I heard the muffled scream as it squeezed through my fingers. And I felt her body thrash against mine. And I noticed her small firm breasts; white and fresh. A warm rush of dark fluid spilled upon them. The blood, wine red and vivid, pumped in vibrant arcs across the table. Like the traces of the world renown fountains that danced outside in the gardens of the Luminous Palace.

The seventeen knifes of my Kameraden had done their duty also. The beautiful dancers of Vienna screamed loudly. The crowd surged in panic as the eighteen bodies fell across the tables with a dull thud. The blood flowed onto the tablecloths. The linen thirstily soaked it up. Just as the very drunkards had greedily supped and soaked up the blood red wine.

'And so will I treat the enemies of my Emperor… and thus I will maintain the stability of his rule.'

The Warlord turned to the Great Emperor and

bowed his head as he clicked both the heels of his thigh length leather boots together. The Great Emperor rose. He nodded to the Warlord and left the room. The Queen Regent escorted him. The High Priest followed them.

The blood of the Great Emperor's half brothers and half sisters, cousins, and cousins once, and twice removed, indeed all the families relations, spread across the feasting tables. They left behind huge red stains which leaked like a dark sea on to the brilliantly patterned marble floor.

The Warlord stood at the high table reconnoitring the scene. He lazily smiled his gentle half smile as he watched the room swiftly empty.

★

It had been a memorable return to Munich for its notorious exiled lord. Named Louis; yet called Ludwig by his countrymen. The Duke of Bavaria, Count Palatine of the Rhine, was a true born nephew of Henry the Lion and a direct lineal descendant of the Old Kings of High Österriech.

He was a warrior, a husband, a father, a murderer, and to some a thief…but to most he would always be simply…Lud The Black

Disclaimer

This novel is a work of fiction which takes place in a fantasy world. A substantial amount of imagination and creativity has been employed to ensure that any similarity between names, characters, businesses, places, events, incidents, actual persons, alive or dead, in your world are completely and purely coincidental.

More Information

More information on the Alchemy Series, The Great Book of Alchemy, all the 5th Worlde Sagas and other related matter is available at the website.

http://www.5thworlde.com
&
http:// greatbookofalchemy.com

Also by the Author

The following books by the author are also available.

Alchemy Series

Book 1
The Work of Gods

Book 2
The Adventures of Robyn Nudd ~ Part I
 Whole Heap O'Troubles

Book 3
The Worst Hero ~ Part I
The Rise of Germania

www.ingramcontent.com/pod-product-compliance
Lightning Source LLC
Chambersburg PA
CBHW070453170726
48291CB00005B/1734